The Inside Name

By Randi Sonenshine

Illustrated by Gina Capaldi

APPLES & HONEY PRESS

A Note from PJ Library®

Jews had a long history of living peacefully in Spain and Portugal, creating a cultural "golden age" between 900 and 1200 CE. But during the era of the Inquisition, from 1478 to 1834, Jews had to live a double life: They needed to appear Christian on the outside, even as they remained Jewish on the inside. These hidden Jews are often called crypto-Jews or conversos to indicate that they had changed their religion. They continued to practice Jewish rituals, risking terrible punishment. That's why Samuel's parents cover the mezuzah and hide their Shabbat candles. One glimpse of these Jewish ritual items by the authorities, and the family might have ended up in Lisbon's jail like Samuel's friend Solomon.

Samuel's papa says, "Words may sting, but they won't kill us." Samuel has to remind himself of this when someone calls him a marrano, Spanish for "pig"–a classic antisemitic slur. Antisemitism existed long before the Inquisition era, and unfortunately it still exists around the world today. For Samuel, injustices like being called a bad name or being chased by the mean Alvarez brothers hurt even more because he loves where he lives. Luckily, Samuel and his family will soon be able to head for a new place that they will hopefully come to love as well.

Samuel's family escapes Portugal with the assistance of courageous friends. Father Tomás and La Señora (Doña Gracia Nasi) find ways to work around the political system in order to deliver fellow Jews to safety. Jews and non-Jews throughout history have bravely found ways to be helpers in dangerous situations. Thanks to Father Tomás and La Señora, Samuel embarks on an adventure to "explore distant lands," just as he had always imagined. This voyage, like many other journeys that Jews have taken over the centuries, will bring his family freedom and redemption in a new land.

A Note from PJ Library®

Hands On!

Doña Gracia Nasi sends Father Tomás a secret message on a scroll that Samuel hides under his hat. You can send a secret message the same way.

Supplies:
- a small piece of paper
- a marker or a pen
- a sticker or piece of tape

Write a secret message on the paper and sign it with a code name. Roll the paper up tightly, then seal it with a sticker or piece of tape. Put the scroll in your pocket or under your hat and deliver it to the right person!

About PJ Library

The gift of PJ Library is made possible by thousands of generous supporters, your Jewish community, the PJ Library Alliance, and the Harold Grinspoon Foundation. PJ Library shares Jewish culture and values through quality children's books that reflect the diversity of Jewish customs and practice. To learn more about the program and ways to connect to local activities, visit **pjlibrary.org**.

Secrets

Outside, I am called Felipe Alonso. But inside, I have a secret name.

In the late afternoon, when the red clay tiles of our roof have been baked warm by the Lisbon sun, I scramble to the top and pretend I am king of Portugal. I survey my land to the south. From the rooftop, the Tagus River gleams like a blue satin ribbon dotted with the white sails of merchant ships.

If I were king, I would not sit fat and happy in my palace on the hill. I would have my pick of the great **caravels** that crowd the port of Lisbon, and their tall masts would carry my banner of gold and red.

Caravel: Spanish/Portuguese sailing ships.

Like Prince **Henry the Navigator**, I would explore distant lands, where birds of every color roost in the trees and yellow-eyed tigers crouch in the tall grass.

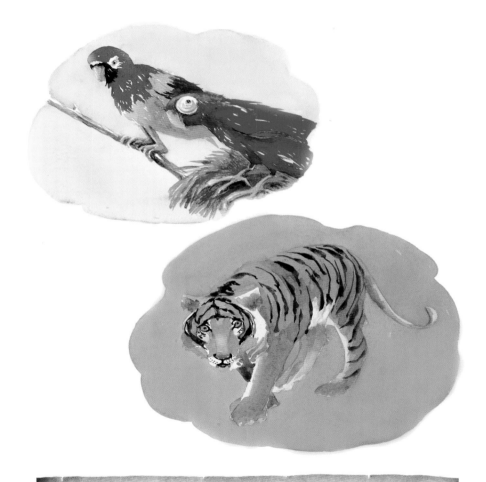

Prince Henry the Navigator: A sponsor of many Portuguese voyages of discovery in the fifteenth century.

Suddenly, Mama's secret whistle brings me back from faraway lands. It is her way of calling me without having to use my outside name.

If I were king, I wouldn't need an outside name. I would be called by my Jewish name all the time. On Friday evenings, Mama could place the Sabbath candles

in the window for all to see, instead of hiding them in the big clay jar by the hearth.

Papa could write his beautiful Hebrew poetry by the light of day. He wouldn't have to wait until the moon paints the church spires silver, and then hide each slender scroll under the loose floorboard in his study.

But we are conversos—Jews who had been forced to convert to Christianity. Some, like us, continue to practice our true faith in secret. But we are always under suspicion, and getting caught would mean terrible punishment.

I think of my best friend Solomon. That was his inside name.

If I were king, I would free him and his parents from jail and send away the hooded men who took them there. And Solomon would be next to me on the warm roof right now, instead of locked away in a cold monastery with only the sour-faced monks for company.

Mama whistles again, louder this time. I scoot to the edge of the roof and shimmy down the sturdy branches of our olive tree into the courtyard, where she is waiting with a basket of lemons. I breathe in their sweet smell.

"Take these to Father Tomás," she says. She tries to smile, but I can feel the worry behind her words. Kissing me on the top of my head, she walks me to the iron gate. I know her dark eyes will follow me until she can see me no more.

2

A Mysterious Mission

The walk to St. Vincent's is not far, but the cobblestone streets are narrow, and the tall, whitewashed buildings throw shadow monsters across my path. Merchant Street is crowded with craftsmen's stalls and workshops. Before the **Inquisition** came, I loved these streets. Now a hundred pairs of eyes seem to watch me.

> **Inquisition:** An institution of the Catholic Church that brutally punished those suspected of continuing Jewish practices in secret.

As I walk by Diego the knife grinder, he stops his squeaky spinning wheel and glares at me with yellowed eyes. "**Marrano**," he grunts and spits at my feet.

It is a hateful word—"pig." I quicken my steps and turn my eyes to the pebbled ground. Diego's cruel laugh follows me. Shame burns on my cheeks and fear sits in my stomach like a rotten melon.

Then I remember what Papa told me. "Words may sting, but they won't kill us." I lift my head and walk on.

Marrano: Literally "pig" in Spanish. Used as a derogatory term for Jews who converted to Catholicism but who practiced their Judaism in secret.

Inside St. Vincent's chapel, it is dark and quiet. Finding myself alone, I whisper the prayer Papa taught me the day I learned my inside name. "I enter this house, but I worship not sticks and stones, only the God of Israel." Papa said it meant that God's form is a mystery, and we cannot contain it in an object, like a wooden cross or a golden statue, no matter how precious the material.

I find Father Tomás in the vestry, where the sacred objects for Mass are kept. Smiling, he puts down the silver chalice he has been polishing and greets me with a hug that smells of incense and oranges. He places his hands on my head and blesses me in Hebrew. Father Tomás is a converso too.

"Ah, the sweetest lemons in Lisbon," he says in a low voice, spying my basket. "Did you know that your lemon tree grew from a cutting that your grandfather, of blessed memory, carried all the way here from **Castile** when Jews were forced to leave Spain?"

I nod. "Every Passover, at our secret seder, Papa tells that story. He says it is the tale of *our* family's Exodus."

Castile: A historical region of central Spain.

"True," Father Tomás says, placing his hands on my shoulders. "And your grandfather carried more than the lemon cutting on that terrible journey. At times, he even carried some people who were tired and weak. He helped them leave Spain."

"He did?" I ask.

"Indeed!" he says. "Your grandfather had the courage of the biblical Joshua. Still, many other Jews died along the way." Father Tomás shakes his bald head sadly and sighs. Then, after a moment, he smiles and pats me on the shoulder.

"But your grandfather's lemon tree flourishes," he says, with a twinkle in his eyes. Glancing quickly around the room, he lowers his voice even more. "As will our people long after the flames of the Inquisition have died. I am sure of it. And you and your family shall be among them."

He takes the basket of lemons and hands me a small, gold pouch in return. It feels silky and mysterious in my hands. Something inside rustles.

"What is it?" I ask.

"You will know soon," he says, removing my blue velvet hat. He places the pouch inside the silky rim before putting the hat back on my head. It feels strange but not uncomfortable.

"Go straight home and give it to your father. Look sharp on the way and show it to no one. I dare not deliver it myself, lest I be discovered. Who, then, would carry on this important work?"

He places both hands on my shoulders and whispers, "I must continue in secrecy. But not you, Felipe. Soon you will have no need of an outside name."

3

A Race from Danger

I hurry home, forcing myself not to run up the steep, winding lanes. The pouch seems to rustle louder with each step, and I fear its shape is visible under the soft fabric of my hat. I hold my breath as I near Diego's stall, but his wheel is silent. Whispering a prayer of thanks, I continue on.

When I get to the corner, I pause at Solomon's house. Through the open gate, I see the garden overgrown with weeds, and I wonder what happened to his brown dog, Poco. I look up at the house. All of the shutters are closed. The one by Solomon's window is chipped on the corner, where I threw a pebble to wake him one morning. It was the day of the royal parade of ships.

That day, Solomon and I had been waiting forever to see King John III's new ship, the *Botafogo*, the most powerful in the world.

At the harbor that day, we ran alongside the mighty ship until we were out of breath, trying to count its many gleaming cannons. We stood atop barrels to watch the rest of the parade. As the ships sailed into the mouth of the great ocean, we cheered with all of

Lisbon. Then cannons boomed out a final salute from the Belém Tower. It had been one of our greatest adventures together. But now Solomon and his family were locked away in Belém's **monastery**.

Monastery: A building where religious people called monks live and worship.

I turn at the sound of voices. Two boys make their way up the street, kicking a ball. I recognize two of them. They are the Alvarez brothers, Luis and Gaspar, the meanest boys in the village. Last spring, they threw rotten meat at Solomon and me on our way back from the market. It took Mama three washings to get the smell out of my clothes.

Fearing they might catch up to me, I check my hat to make sure the cargo is secure and start quickly in the direction of my house.

Before I have gone far, someone yells, "Get him!" I begin to run. The hidden pouch slides around, and I fear my hat will slip off and reveal my secret. I hold it tight to my head with one hand. My house is just around the next corner, but they are almost upon me. I turn sharply to cut through the fruit seller's yard. My heart thumps as I hurdle baskets of pears, plums, and dates. Finally, my gate is in sight. I sprint the last few feet and dart into the safety of my own courtyard, locking the gate behind me.

4

A Way Out

After I catch my breath, I enter the doorway, pausing to brush my fingers over the third blue tile above the latch. Beneath it is our family's mezuzah, a small scroll on which is written Judaism's most sacred prayer, the Sh'ma. It is our secret way of observing the Jewish law to keep a mezuzah upon our doorpost.

Suddenly, a thought strikes me. I wonder if Solomon's

nosy neighbor, Señora Pinto, spied him touching the place where his family's sacred mezuzah was hidden as he entered his house. Is that why the men in hoods took his family away? And if it happened to them, could it happen to my family?

I shake off the terrible thought and go inside. In the kitchen, Mama is kneading a fluffy ball of dough. She hugs me with floured hands, then pinches off a small piece of dough to occupy my little sister, Beatriz, who is still too young to know her inside name. In silence, Mama follows me into Papa's study.

Papa sits hunched over his desk, his quill scritch-scratching across a piece of parchment. The shelves above his head are lined with worn books, inkpots, and an assortment of quills. They are the tools of his work as a scribe and translator for nobles and wealthy villagers. "It is not poetry, but at least I am writing," he always says.

He looks up and calls me to him. The sound of my inside name is sweet music. I long to hear it all the time.

"From Father Tomás," I say, removing the silky pouch from my hat.

Carefully, Papa withdraws from the pouch a scroll and breaks the dark blue seal. The parchment is thick and creamy, with neat rows of perfectly curled script. As Papa reads, I see a new light in his eyes. When he finishes, he smiles and hugs Mama. "Our prayers have been answered," he says.

"La Señora?" Mama asks.

Papa nods in reply. Mama hugs him. There are tears in her eyes, but I know it is because she is happy.

"Who is La Señora?" I ask.

"Beatriz de Luna Mendes," Papa says. "She rules a trading empire and has many ships that bring pepper and other spices from the East. She and her family have helped many of our people escape the claws of the Inquisition."

"But, Papa," I ask. "Why does she want to help us?"

"Her inside name is Gracia Nasi," says Papa. "She is a converso too."

"Will we get to go on a big ship?" I ask.

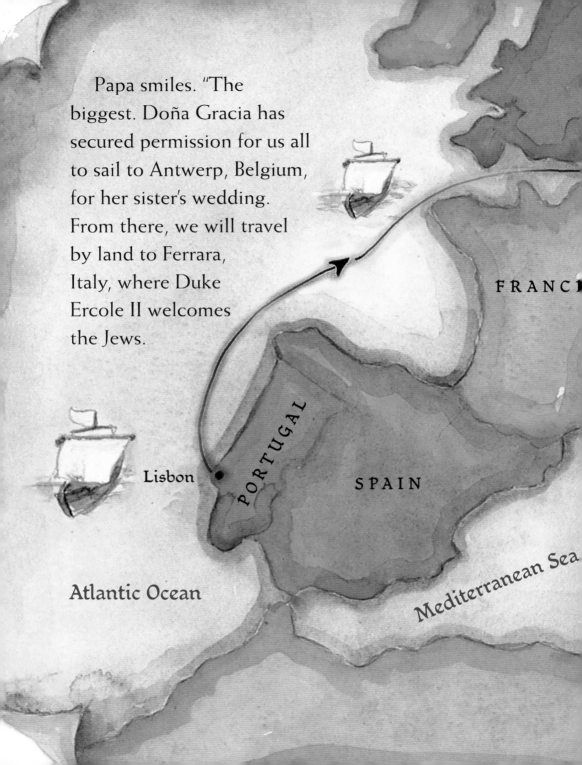

Papa smiles. "The biggest. Doña Gracia has secured permission for us all to sail to Antwerp, Belgium, for her sister's wedding. From there, we will travel by land to Ferrara, Italy, where Duke Ercole II welcomes the Jews.

FRANCE

Lisbon

PORTUGAL

SPAIN

Atlantic Ocean

Mediterranean Sea

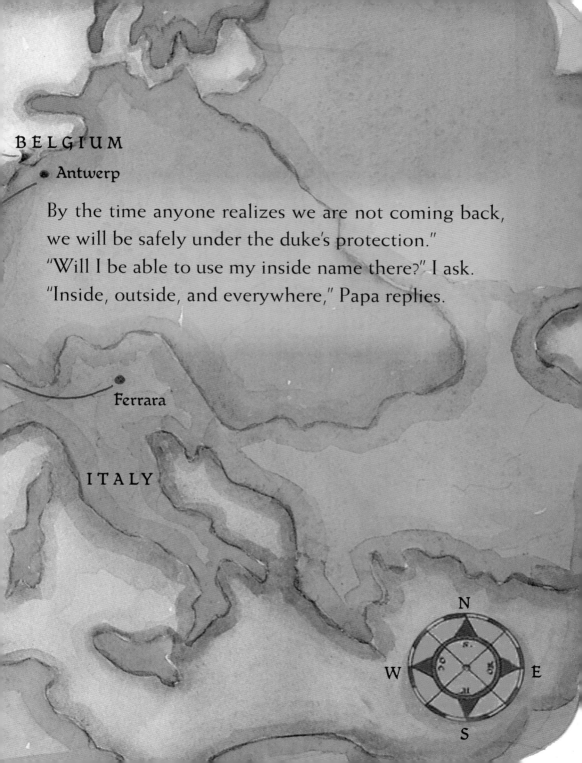

BELGIUM

• Antwerp

By the time anyone realizes we are not coming back,
we will be safely under the duke's protection."
"Will I be able to use my inside name there?" I ask.
"Inside, outside, and everywhere," Papa replies.

• Ferrara

ITALY

N

W   E

S

5

The Two Kings

All the next week, we prepare for the trip. It is hard to choose just a few things to take, knowing we will never return, but we must look as if we are leaving for only a short time. In a secret compartment of our trunk, Mama hides her Sabbath candlesticks, Papa's poetry, and the mezuzah she sneaked out from under the blue tile in our doorway. I search my treasures, wondering what to choose, but I cannot decide.

On the day before our departure, I still have not decided, so I seek out Papa for wisdom. I find him in his study. He stands silently in the middle of the room staring at his desk. On the desktop, books are stacked neatly, and a quill rests quietly in its stand. Behind the desk, rolls of creamy parchment peek from shadowed cubbies and ink bottles line a worn, wooden shelf like round-bellied monks. It looks as it always has, and not as if we are about to leave forever. Papa's shoulders droop, and I wonder if that is what he is thinking too. It seems wrong to disturb him, so I leave him with his thoughts.

Back in my room, I take another look around. What will I miss the most?

When I spy the chess set Solomon gave me for my birthday last spring, I know I have finally found the answer. Before I give it to Mama for packing, I find the two kings and slip them into my pocket. It gives me comfort to feel them there together.

At last, the day of the voyage arrives. While Papa loads our belongings into the carriage that will take us to the waterfront, I climb onto the roof one last

time. It is early morning, and the clay tiles are not yet warm. Down below, on the Tagus River, the sails of the merchant ships are shrouded in a soft mist. Soon I will be on one of those majestic ships bound for a new land, like the great explorers.

I look out toward Solomon's house for the last time, and my eyes fill up with tears. I wrap my hand tightly around the two wooden kings in my pocket and let their solid warmth comfort me.

Papa calls from below. With a final glance over the sea of red rooftops, I wipe away my tears and climb down into the courtyard. Suddenly, the sweet smell of lemons surrounds me, and I know what I must do.

6

Sailing to Freedom

I hurry to the house and head straight to Papa's study, where I find one of the small knives he uses to sharpen his quills. In the kitchen, I grab a clean cloth, dip it in the water jar, and sprint back to the courtyard.

"Felipe!" Father calls. "The captain does not wait for dawdling young boys!"

"Coming!" I answer, as I reach Grandfather's lemon

tree. Thick with ripe fruit, the branches hang low enough for me to reach. Carefully, I cut off a small stem with several fragrant, glossy leaves and wrap the cut end in the wet cloth. When I slip it into my pocket, I pull out one of the chess kings.

Holding the warm wooden piece, I think about the many times Solomon and I played here under the cool canopy of leaves. When tears come again, I dig a small hole with Papa's knife, and gently lay in the king. As I cover it with the soft earth, I whisper a quick prayer that Solomon and his parents will be released soon, and that we will play together again someday. Then, I take a deep breath, place a fallen leaf over the small mound, and hurry to the waiting carriage.

Finally, we board the ship. Up close, the caravel is even more magnificent than I imagined. While Mama and Beatriz find our sleeping quarters, Papa and I watch the crew ready the boat for departure. I see Papa glance anxiously at the shore, and I know he fears that someone will yet try to stop us. I take his hand and tell him not to worry. Just as Grandfather did, we will have the biblical Joshua's courage to help us on our journey. Then he hugs me, and we both smile.

Mama and Beatriz return to the deck. With a great lurch, we begin to move through the crowded river toward the mouth of the Great Green Ocean. Clutching the lemon stem in my hands, I remember Father Tomás's words. I know that, like Grandfather's tree, my family will flourish in our new land.

As the sails of the caravel blossom in the wind, and the city of Lisbon slips away, I whisper goodbye to my outside name.

Soon, like my grandfather and his grandfather before him, I will be called Samuel.

Historical Note

Although Samuel's story is fictional, the setting and situations are based on real history. In 1496, Portugal's King Manuel I forced all the Jews in his kingdom to convert to Christianity and forbade them from leaving the country. Many of these converted Jews, called conversos, maintained a secret Jewish life inside their homes. They met in cellars or hidden rooms to pray and observe the Sabbath and other Jewish holidays, such as Passover. They adopted secret symbols, gestures, and rituals to maintain their Judaism while outwardly appearing Christian. One of these practices was to have two names. While outside or in church, they usually used the name of a saint or another Christian name. However, in the safety of their homes, or when in the company of other conversos, they used a Hebrew or Jewish name. They lived in constant fear of being discovered. If caught practicing Judaism, they faced imprisonment and possibly death.

Help came in the form of Doña Gracia Nasi, a wealthy Portuguese converso who ran a shipping and trading empire. Doña Gracia, or La Señora, as the Jewish people came to call her, was a brilliant businesswoman and tough negotiator, who used her wealth and powerful connections throughout Europe to operate a secret escape network for her fellow Jews. She smuggled them onto her spice ships and provided guides, safe houses, money, and supplies to get them first to Italy, and then to Ottoman Empire Greece or Turkey, where they were free to practice Judaism.

Doña Gracia eventually settled in Turkey, where she built synagogues and Jewish schools, organized and funded assistance for the needy, and resettled the incoming refugees. She even persuaded the sultan of the Ottoman Empire, Suleiman the Magnificent, to gift her the city of Tiberias in the Holy Land, so she could create a haven for Jews.

Because of her wisdom, strength, and generosity, thousands of conversos, like Samuel and his family in the story, were finally able to reclaim their Jewish identities and live in peace.

Apples & Honey Press • An Imprint of Behrman House Publishers
Millburn, New Jersey 07041
www.applesandhoneypress.com
Printed in China

ISBN 978-1-68115-619-4

Text copyright © 2023 by Randi Sonenshine • Illustrations copyright © 2023 by Behrman House

First published as a short story by Cricket Media in April 2017 © by Randi Sonenshine. Reproduced with permission

Lexile® 870L

0524/B2527/A8